Useless

by

Tanya Landman

Illustrated by Julia Page

First published in 2007 in Great Britain by
Barrington Stoke Ltd
18 Walker Street, Edinburgh, EH3 7LP

www.barringtonstoke.co.uk

Reprinted 2008

ISBN: 978-1-84299-459-7

Printed in Great Britain by Bell & Bain Ltd

A Note from the Author

Useless is, I think, the most personal book I've ever written. It's a story, so nothing in the book really happened. (My own stepdad never even picked up a ping pong bat, and never won a match with it!).

But the book has its roots in real life. I did have a father who was good looking and funny – and *Useless* in every way! I also had a lovely stepdad, and luckily he was a writer. He showed me that writing is a real job done by real people. He gave me something to aim for. This is my "thank you" to him.

For Roy

Contents

Chapter 1
Torn Apart

Useless. That's what Mum called him.
Useless.

I can't remember what Dad had done.
All I can see is the look on Mum's face. Her
eyes were like little slits, her lips shut tight

as a cat's bum. And that sharp, mocking voice – she could have melted steel with it.

I didn't say a thing. I could never seem to find words to argue with Mum. But I remember the white hot rage inside me.

You see, Dad wasn't useless. I was in Junior School back then, and I knew that Dad was fantastic. The best. No one else had a dad who could swim for 20 metres under water. No one else had a dad who could pull a 50p coin out of your ear.

No one else had a dad who could build a
snowman taller than I was.

He was always laughing. Always cracking jokes.

Dad was magic.

But one day he wasn't there any more.

There was no big drama. No yelling kids dragged away from their weeping dad. There was none of that stuff that you see on TV.

He just went.

At tea-time he was there. The next morning he wasn't.

When she got up, Mum looked pink and puffy. She must have been crying all night.

"He's gone, Rob," was what she said to me. "Dad's not coming back."

And I knew, I just knew she was to blame.

My sister Maggie didn't seem to mind much, but then she was only two, she didn't know what was going on.

I was ten. I was upset. Really upset. And scared. I felt like my world had been torn apart. Like someone had peeled my skin off. Like I'd never be safe again.

But I didn't show it. I didn't say a thing. I shut my mouth tight to stop any words getting out. I didn't say anything to Mum. The only way I could deal with this was by thinking it wasn't true.

I knew Dad would be back.

For weeks and weeks I watched and waited, knowing that one day, Dad would walk through the door, pull a 50p piece out of my ear, and take me off down to the swimming pool like he used to. Even when the weeks turned into months and the months turned into years, I still knew Dad would come back. It got to be a habit.

Chapter 2
The Enemy

When Mark moved in two years later the idea that Dad would come back got harder to hold on to, but I didn't give up. It didn't matter that I hardly ever heard from him. I sometimes got a postcard with "See you soon, Love Dad" on the back and it was all I needed. I knew he was out there, and I knew he'd come home. So I wasn't going to be nice to Mark. No way. I wasn't going to let Dad down.

I didn't even speak to Mark at first. For weeks I acted as if he wasn't there. But it's hard to share a house with someone and *never* talk to them. Sometimes I had to – but it was only stuff like "Pass the ketchup" or "Can I have the salt?" And I had found a way of looking past him as if he wasn't there.

Maggie didn't have any problems. She liked Mark from the start.

One day I came home from school and found her sitting on his lap. They were watching telly. There she was, tucked up all nice and cosy, like she was *his* kid. Mark was sitting in Dad's place – *Dad's* place – as if it was *his* sofa.

It made me sick.

I was going right back out again – I wasn't going to stay in there. But before I

could get to the door Mark jumped up as if I'd spilt boiling hot tea into his lap.

"Hi Rob ... Come and sit down and watch some telly ... I'll go and get the tea," he muttered, and he rushed off to the kitchen like a scared rabbit. And then Mum came home and joined him. Maggie went off to find her, and the next thing I knew they were all out in the kitchen, laughing and joking. I was left sitting on my own watching some stupid cartoon on the telly.

Only I wasn't on my own. Not really. I had Dad with me – in my head. There was his place, the cushion dented by Mark's bum. I got up and shook it out. I didn't go into the kitchen. And when tea was ready, I just took it and ate it in the front room. I wasn't going to be soft on the Enemy.

That was how I saw Mark. As the Enemy. Mark didn't try to change my mind. He never even tried to make friends.

It was funny. My best mate Tom had a new step-mum and she was always trying

to be nice with Tom and his big sister –
taking them off shopping, buying them
stuff, taking them out to see a film.
Flashing the cash seemed to work too. Tom
thought his new step-mum was fantastic.

Mark didn't try any of that stuff.
Shame. I'd have loved saying no to him.

The only thing Mark was good at was
table tennis.

"Drippy girl's game," I muttered. Table
tennis. *Ping pong.* It even *sounds* stupid.

Dad was into football. Watching it, not playing it. "The best game of all," he called it. "A real man's sport." He'd sit in front of the telly when a big match was on and let me pull the rings off his beer cans. Mark looked so wet dancing around in his short white socks at weekends. *Short white socks?* I was so ashamed. Dad would have died before wearing short white socks.

No way could I work out why Mum liked Mark better than Dad. It was weird. Dad was a proper man – an off-down-the-pub-for-a-few-pints-and-a-game-of-pool-with-

my-mates man. Mark was a wine-sipping, book-reading, quiet, ping-pong-playing, wet wimp. What did Mum see in him?

Chapter 3
Peace

One Sunday Mark had this big table tennis match. He'd got to the finals of some oldies' competition. Mum insisted that we all go along to watch him "as a family". She said she'd kill me if I didn't go. Even worse, there would be no more pocket money *ever*.

I hated the idea, but no one can live without pocket money *forever*.

I made sure she knew how I felt, though. Slow, dragging walk all the way to the Sports Centre. Head down. Mouth shut tight. Mum got the picture. It drove her mad.

"Behave yourself," she hissed at me and she banged her handbag against my legs. "Try and look a bit happier."

So I fixed this huge cheesy grin on my face and sat there in the front row grinning like an idiot. If that didn't put Mark off, nothing would.

But that match was a bit of a shock.

Mark wasn't the same person out there. He could move dead fast! He hit the balls so hard they thudded round like bullets. It was great stuff. I had to admit I was impressed. And when he won I just had to cheer with everyone else. You can't help

joining in with a happy crowd. The mood's catching.

When it was all over we went out for a pizza. Mum and Mark were all lovey-dovey which was a bit puke-making. Maggie was dancing around like she was on springs. I didn't jump about, but then I didn't look past Mark either. I had a whole lot of rude remarks worked out in my head – *Table tennis? It stinks. Or should I say pongs?* But I didn't feel like saying any of them now.

Mum fixed me with one of her looks, as if she was testing me out. "Well, Rob," she said. "Aren't you going to say anything to Mark? Come on, love ..."

Mark looked all hot and shy. "Rob doesn't need to say anything," he said.

But I muttered into my pizza, "It was wicked. Nice one."

Mark looked at me. I could feel his eyes burning into the top of my head.

"Thanks, Rob," he said. That was all.

But we both knew it was like peace had been declared.

Then Mark made this stupid joke about him being a wicked stepdad. He said I'd better check he hadn't put poison in my pizza. It wasn't that funny, but we all fell around laughing like complete idiots.

When we got back to the house, I started to think, "Well ... He's not Dad. But he's OK."

It just felt sort of nice. Relaxed.

Easy.

There was a film about to start on the telly, so I went into the front room to switch on.

And froze.

Because Dad was back.

Chapter 4
Beer and Chips

He was sitting there on the sofa. In his place. Mark's place. Dad's place. Sitting there with a can of beer in his hand and a load of empties on the floor by his feet. A plate of chips was on his lap. He looked as if he'd never been away.

My belly skipped.

I felt sick.

And so ashamed. I'd just been *nice* to Mark.

How was I going to explain that to Dad?

There was this long silence. It seemed to go on for ever.

It's funny, looking back on it. I mean, you'd think I'd have been pleased to see him. I'd been waiting for him to come home for nearly three years. I should have been over the moon. Happy. Thrilled.

But it felt all wrong.

Because some part of me was thinking he had a real cheek, walking back in like that without even a phone call. I wasn't going to go over and just hug him as if everything was OK. And there was this stink of stale beer, and fag ends, and greasy old chips. I'd forgotten that smell.

It had left the house at the same time as he did.

I stood there, staring at him.

He stared back at me, a kind of half smile fixed on his face as if he wasn't quite sure it was me. I'd grown a lot in three years. I didn't look the same. He was waiting for me to say something.

I'm not sure what I'd have done next. I didn't get a chance to speak.

Mum came in. She was so shocked she nearly fell over. She took a step back and held on to the door.

"How did you get in?"

Dad held up his keys.

Mum's face fell. "I should have changed the locks ..." she muttered. Then she turned on him. "How dare you?"

Mark was into the room in an instant – like I said, he could move very fast when he wanted to.

33

Dad got up. Chips went everywhere. He swayed a bit, and had to grab hold of the back of the sofa.

"Hello mate." He gave Mark this jolly little wave. "So this is the new boyfriend," he said to Mum. He looked at Mark's short white socks. "Very nice." He grinned. "Just came to see the kids," he said. He made it sound so normal. But it wasn't.

And I could smell the beer on him from way across the room.

Mum was talking softly, but I could tell she was really angry. "You walk out, and three years later you just pop back to see the kids?"

That gave me a shock. I'd always thought Mum had told him to go.

I'd always been sure she was to blame.

"That's OK, isn't it?" asked Dad. "Hey, I bet Mandy's a big girl now."

Mum's voice was cold and sharp. You could have cut yourself on it. "Her name's Maggie. Can't you even get that right?"

Dad shrugged. "They're still my kids."

After that everything went mad.

Mum started yelling at him that it wasn't OK and that there was more to being a dad than just popping in when he felt like it.

There was shouting and tears. It was like something off the telly. Not that I got to see much of it. Mum sent me and Maggie off to the park.

Chapter 5

A Nice Treat

It was a cold day, and the park was empty. Maggie and I went round and round on the roundabout. Not saying anything. I kept tight hold of her hand. Maggie had gone white. She does it when she's upset. I mean, she didn't even know who Dad was. Not really. She thought it was a strange man sitting in her front room. She thought Dad was a burglar. She didn't know why Mum hadn't rung the police.

I thought I was going to be sick. I felt the same as I did when Dad left. I was scared. It felt like the world had been torn apart again.

Like someone had peeled my skin off. Like nothing was safe.

I'd got used to Dad not being there.

He'd left this great wide scar which had healed over. But now he was back, ripping the scar off, opening it all up again, making the blood run. Only this time it was worse because I didn't have the old Dad tucked up inside my head any more. The one I knew would come back. I had lost forever this nice, happy picture of the man who'd pulled 50p's from my ear when I was little.

The dad I'd been missing for three years didn't exist. I'd made him up out of a few happy memories.

And all the other memories – the ones
that I'd hidden away for ages – started to
come back. Round and round we went on
that roundabout, me keeping tight hold of
Maggie's hand, while pictures of Dad
flashed inside my head.

The time he'd taken me out to buy me a
new pair of shoes and come back with a
bottle of whisky instead. The time he said
he'd take me to Disneyland. Then the next
day he swore blind that he'd never said it.
The time he got so drunk watching an

England match on the telly that he passed out before the winning goal was scored.

I remembered Mum's face getting more old and grey each time he let her down. Mum looking worn out, with eyes like little slits to stop the tears from falling. And that acid tone of voice – I suddenly saw that it wasn't scorn. It was sadness.

"Useless ... Useless."

I'd been so angry with her. It had been safer to be angry with Mum than face up to the truth. Dad was magic – some of the time. But it wasn't OK to be magic for just some of the time. Mum was right. She'd been right all along. Dad *was* useless.

In the end it was Mark who came to fetch us back. Mum was at home crying her eyes out. It felt as if we'd been sitting on that roundabout for days.

We walked home side by side. Mark reached out to me very gently as if I was a boiling kettle and he might get burnt. He

put his hand on my arm. I didn't push it off.

"Fancy a game of table tennis before tea?" he asked.

"Yeah," I said. "OK."

I could see just why Mum liked Mark. Mark was there. Solid. Mark was a grown-up. She could trust him.

And me. I felt like I'd got a few years older that day.

Maybe I'd started to grow up too. If only Dad would.

"Is he still there?" I asked Mark.

"No," he said. "He's gone. But he's left his address, so you can write to him. And he says he'll come back. He'd like to take you out for a day. A nice treat, a football match or something. He's missed you, he says. He really wants to see you."

I nodded. I didn't say anything. Mark was being nice. I didn't tell him what Dad was like. I was only just seeing it myself.

"A nice treat?" I thought. "Huh!"

****

That was three years ago.

I'm still waiting.

Barrington Stoke would like to thank all its readers for commenting on the manuscript before publication and in particular:

Jack Barker

Kimberley Bull

Jayde Cahill

Gary Cameron

Graham Casement

Danielle Deakins

Christopher Freestone

Lewis Gibb

Samantha Leach

Elizabeth Mair

Gayna Perry

Kerry

Bradley Tiller

Mr Rudd

Chelsea Rudge

Kayleigh Strachan

Bradley Tiller

Lee Tose

Connor Woods

Become a Consultant!

Would you like to give us feedback on our titles before they are published? Contact us at the address below – we'd love to hear from you!

Email: info@barringtonstoke.co.uk
Website: www.barringtonstoke.co.uk

More exciting NEW titles ...

Stray

by

David Belbin

EVEN IN A GANG,

SHE'S ON HER OWN.

Stray's in with the wrong lot.

Can Kev save her?

Or will she drag him down?

gr8reads

More exciting NEW titles ...

Perfect
by
Joanna Kenrick

Too Good To Be True?

Dan and Kate are perfect together.

Nothing can go wrong.

Until the lying starts ...

You can order *Perfect* directly from our website
at **www.barringtonstoke.co.uk**

More exciting NEW titles ...

Shark!
by
Michaela Morgan

Mark knows about sharks.

He knows how they think, live and hunt.

He doesn't know there's a hungry shark
out there, right now.

And it's coming his way ...

You can order *Shark!* directly from our website at
www.barringtonstoke.co.uk